PJMASKS
PJ Masks
Make Friends!

Based on the episode "Catboy's Butterfly Brigade"

Simon Spotlight
New York London Toronto Sydney New Delhi

SIMON SPOTLIGHT
An imprint of Simon & Schuster Children's Publishing Division
1230 Avenue of the Americas, New York, New York 10020
First Simon Spotlight paperback edition December 2016
This book is based on the TV series PJ MASKS © Frog Box / Entertainment One UK Limited / Walt Disney EMEA Productions Limited 2014;
Les Pyjamasques by Romuald © (2007) Gallimard Jeunesse. All Rights Reserved.
This book/publication © Entertainment One UK Limited 2016.
Adapted by Cala Spinner from the series PJ Masks
All rights reserved, including the right of reproduction in whole or in part in any form.
SIMON SPOTLIGHT and colophon are registered trademarks of Simon & Schuster, Inc.
For information about special discounts for bulk purchases, please contact Simon & Schuster Special Sales at 1-866-506-1949 or business@simonandschuster.com.
Manufactured in the United States of America 0617 LAK
10 9 8 7 6 5 4 3
ISBN 978-1-4814-8907-2 (pbk)
ISBN 978-1-4814-8908-9 (eBook)

Connor, Greg, and Amaya are visiting the zoo.

"Greg and I want to see the butterflies," Amaya says.

"Butterflies?" Connor says. "No way! They just flap around. I want to see the big cats—with their big teeth and claws!" He jumps up and roars.

"Connor! Stop being so rough," Amaya says. "*We* want to see the butterflies. We can all go and see the lions and tigers later."

Disappointed, Connor follows Greg and Amaya to the butterfly house. But the butterfly house is empty!

"The butterflies are *gone*!" Amaya cries.

"PJ Masks, we're on our way! Into the night to save the day!"
Amaya becomes Owlette!
Greg becomes Gekko!
Connor becomes Catboy!

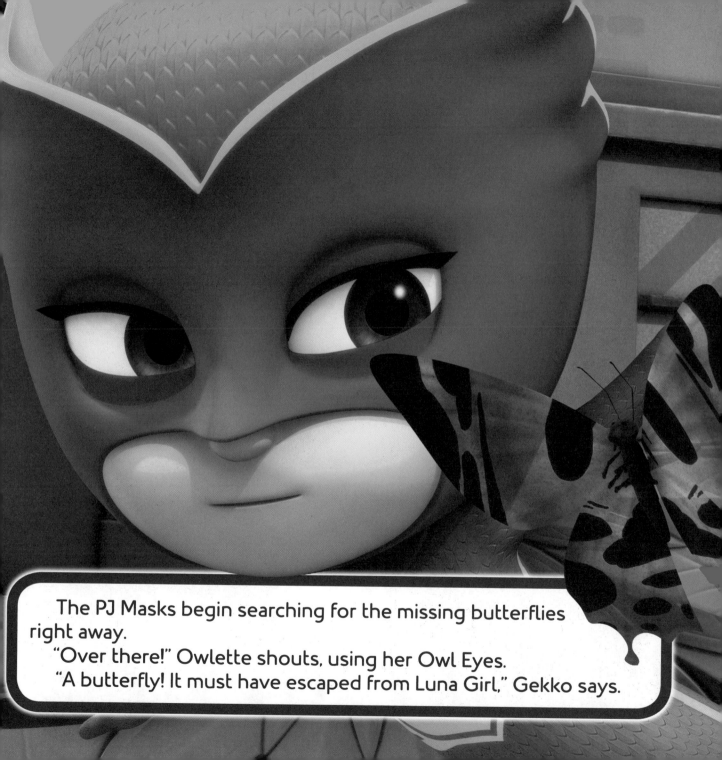

The PJ Masks begin searching for the missing butterflies right away.

"Over there!" Owlette shouts, using her Owl Eyes.

"A butterfly! It must have escaped from Luna Girl," Gekko says.

Gekko and Owlette try to convince the butterfly to come with them. Owlette asks the butterfly if it wants to fly with her. Gekko changes his colors to match the butterfly's wings.

"This is taking too long," Catboy complains. "What we need is some . . . *Super Cat Speed*!"

In a flash, Catboy grabs a small net and a box with some holes in it. He zips around Gekko and Owlette and shoves the lonely butterfly into the box.

"You were really rough, Catboy," Owlette says. "You're making it unhappy."

"But this is the best way to get it home," Catboy says. "And there are more to catch. Look! *Super Cat Speed!*"

Catboy zooms toward the butterflies with his net!

The box shimmies and shakes on the ground. "Catboy! Can't you be gentle? You're making those butterflies really miserable!" Owlette says.

"But I'm *helping* them," Catboy says. "Now, where's Luna Girl with the others?"

Suddenly, the PJ Masks see a cloud of moths in the sky.
"Fly away!" a voice near them shouts. "I don't need you anymore."
It's Luna Girl!
"You've messed up enough, measly moths—time to try some new *butterfly* sidekicks," she says.

"Not so fast, Luna Girl! The PJ Masks are here to take those butterflies back!" says Catboy.

Luna Girl looks at her moths.

"Oh, all right, moths. *One* last chance—get rid of these PJ pests!" she tells them.

The moths swarm around Owlette and Gekko.

Luna Girl sets her eyes on Catboy.
"Get him, Butterfly Brigade," she tells the butterflies, "or you'll be trapped by my Luna–Magnet forever!"
The butterflies zoom toward Catboy.

Quickly, he uses his net to capture the butterflies. But they don't like being caught. Some of them escape!

"Whoa! Where do you think you're going?" Catboy asks. He accidentally knocks over the box with the rest of the butterflies . . . and now they *all* escape!

Catboy tries recapturing the butterflies with his net.
"Stop being so rough!" Owlette calls out.
But it's too late—the butterflies are mad. They push Catboy, and he falls down, hard.

"Take *that*, Catboy!" Luna Girl shouts triumphantly. She turns to the moths. "See, you useless moths, *that's* how it's done!"

Catboy is confused. "But I was trying to save the butterflies," he says.
"Maybe they're angry at being put in a box," Gekko suggests.
"No one likes being shoved around," Owlette says. "Did *you?*"

Catboy realizes that Gekko and Owlette are right.
"I *was* rough with them," he admits. "But when they were rough with me, I didn't like it at all!"

Luna Girl points a finger at the PJ Masks.
"Go on, Butterfly Brigade! Get them!"
But the butterflies swarm her instead.
"They don't like Luna Girl being rough with them, either!" Catboy realizes. "It's time to be a hero!"

Catboy leaps up and uses his *Super Cat Speed*! With a flash of blue light, he gathers a bunch of flowers for the butterflies to eat.

"I'm really sorry about before, butterflies," Catboy says. "I've brought you as many flowers as I could find. *Please* come with us. . . ."

One butterfly lands on a flower. Then the rest follow!

"Wait! Butterflies—you can't go with them!" Luna Girl calls out. But the butterflies continue to follow the PJ Masks—and her moths do, too!

"No! No! No! Now I haven't got *any* helpers." Luna Girl sniffles. "I'm sorry, moths."

Luna Girl was rough to her moths, so they left her. But now that she is being gentle, her moths return to her side.

Catboy realizes that being nice and gentle is how you make friends. And today, the PJ Masks made lots of friends!
PJ Masks all shout hooray! 'Cause in the night, we saved the day!